PENGUIN BOOKS

THE INSPECTOR

"Mr. Steinberg remains one of the most surprising and inspired artists on the current scene. He is at once a sharp and witty observer of the social scene and—what is quite different—a brilliant commentator on the internal dynamics of the artistic imagination. His art is thus full of marvelous details drawn from the social arena, and equally full of dazzling evocations of the way the form-making faculties of visual imagination act upon the received materials of ordinary life. His art is at once a satire on and a lyric celebration of these usually separate polarities of experience."
—Hilton Kramer, *The New York Times*

STEINBERG

The INSPECTOR

Penguin Books

Penguin Books Ltd, Harmondsworth, Middlesex, England
Penguin Books, 625 Madison Avenue, New York, New York 10022, U.S.A.
Penguin Books Australia Ltd, Ringwood, Victoria, Australia
Penguin Books Canada Ltd, 41 Steelcase Road West, Markham, Ontario, Canada
Penguin Books (N.Z.) Ltd, 182–190 Wairau Road, Auckland 10, New Zealand

First published by The Viking Press 1973
Published in Penguin Books 1976

LIBRARY OF CONGRESS CATALOGING IN PUBLICATION DATA
Steinberg, Saul.
The Inspector.

1. American wit and humor, Pictorial.   I.   Title.
[NC1429.S588A47   1976]   741.5'973   76-18698
ISBN 0 14 00.4285 7

Printed in the United States of America by
The Murray Printing Company, Forge Village, Massachusetts

Most of these drawings originally appeared in *The New Yorker*.

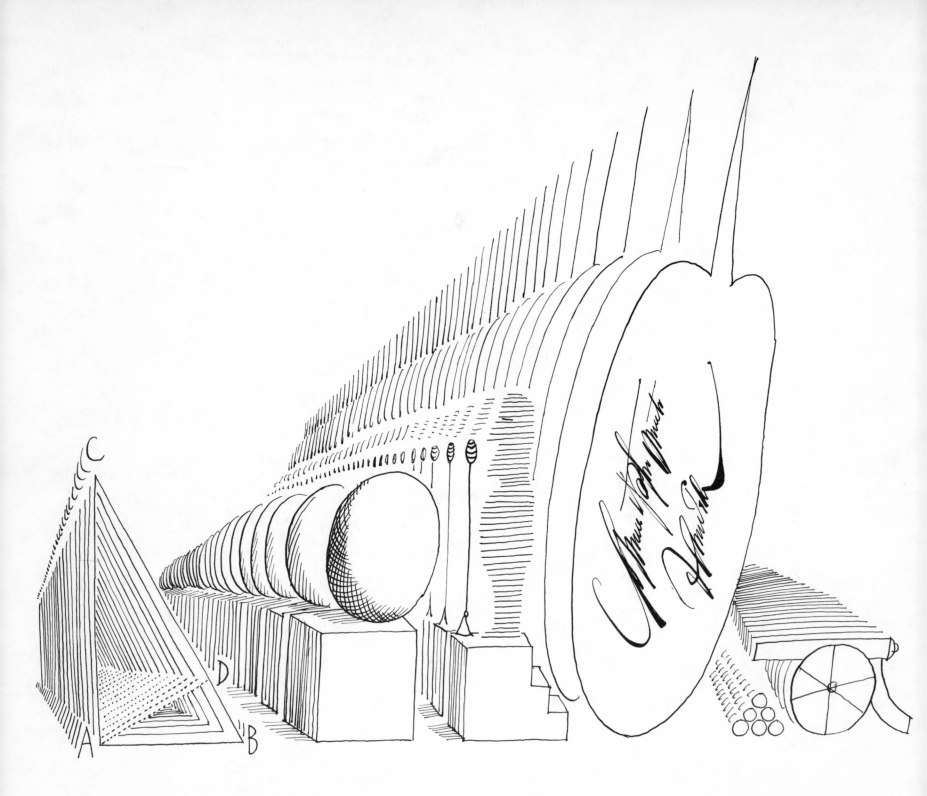

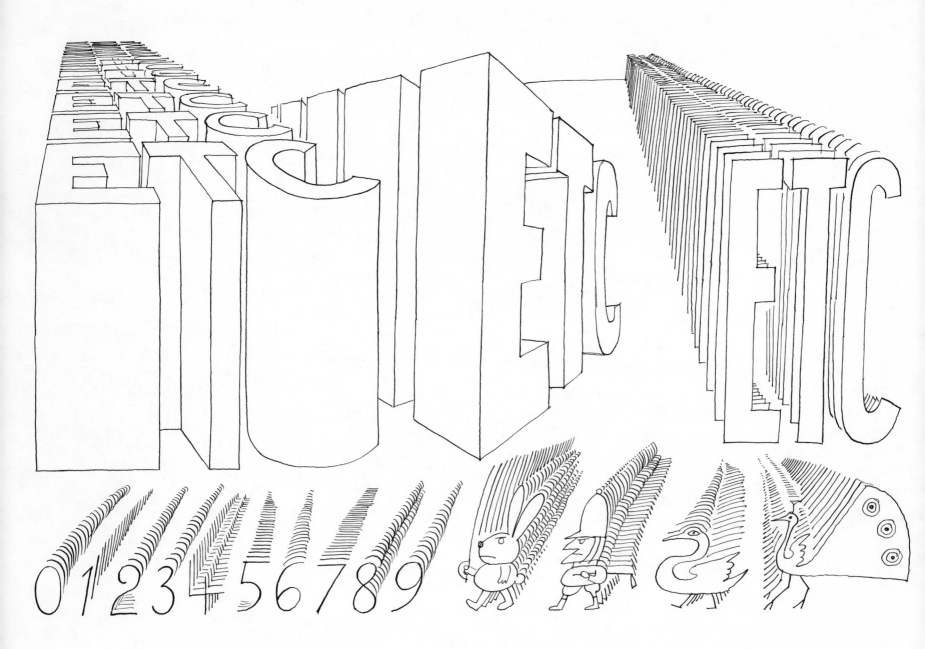

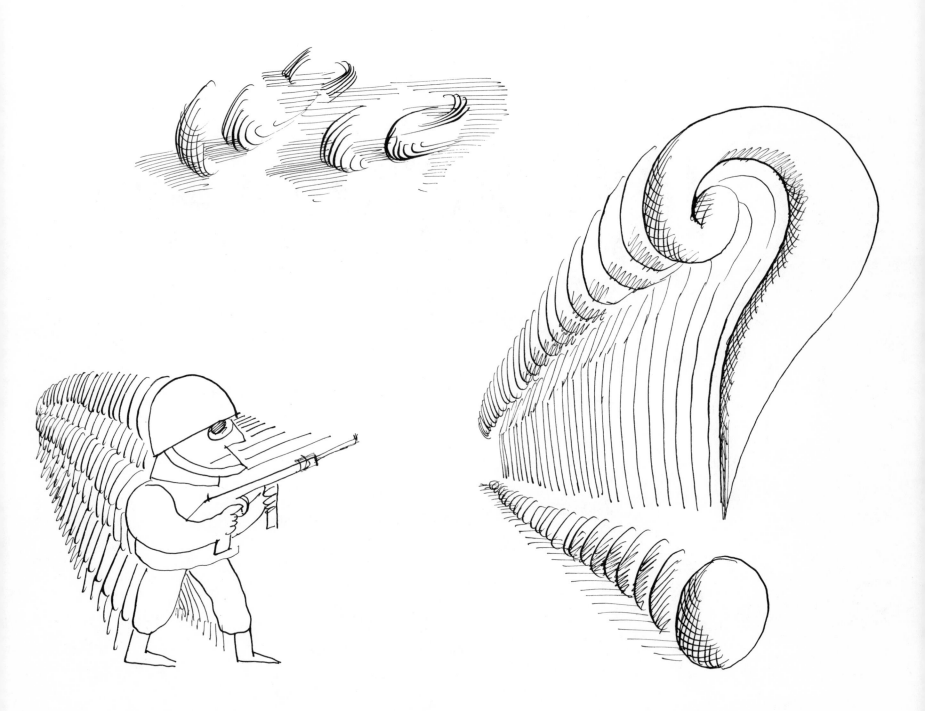

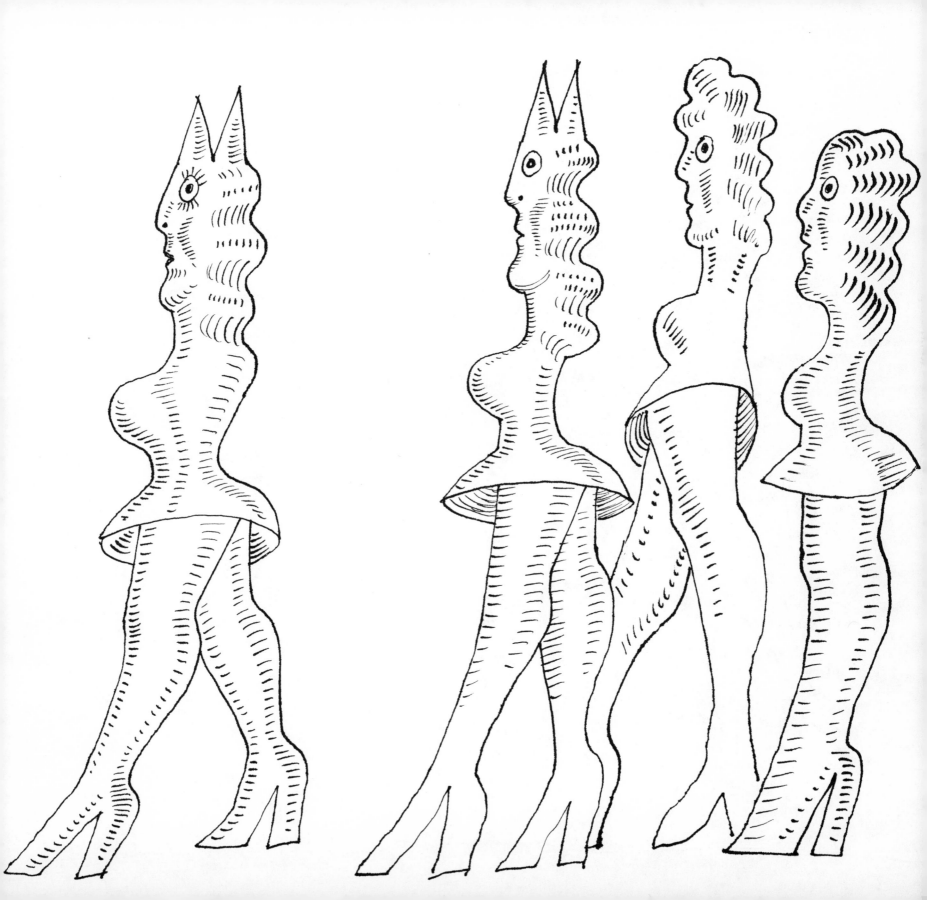

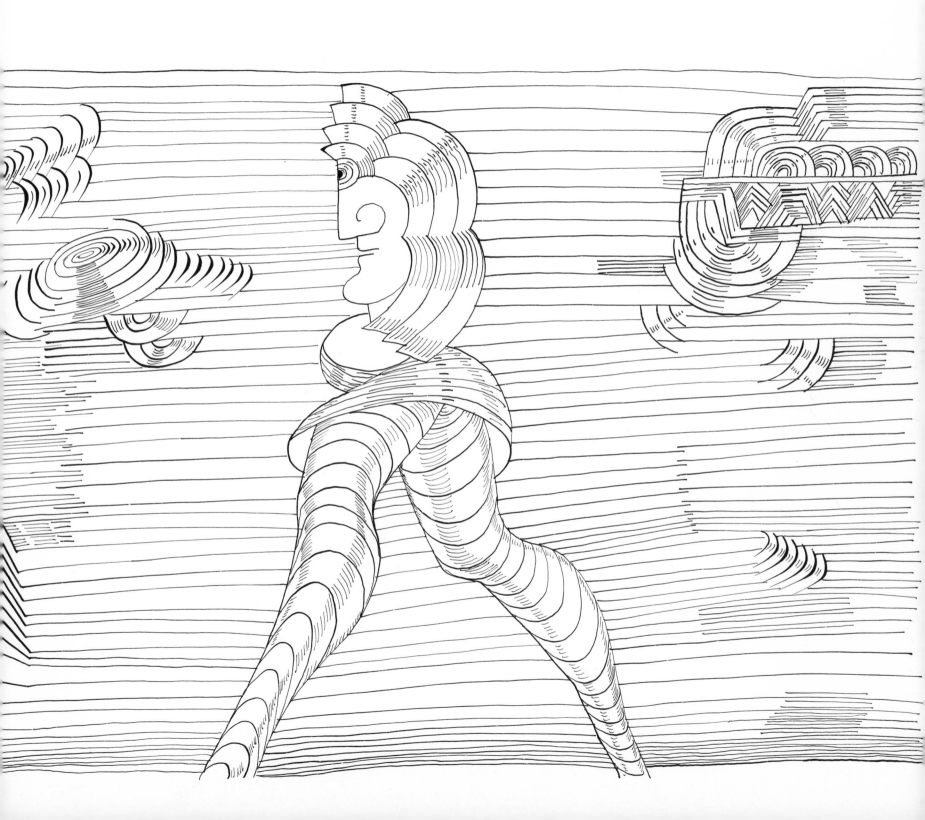

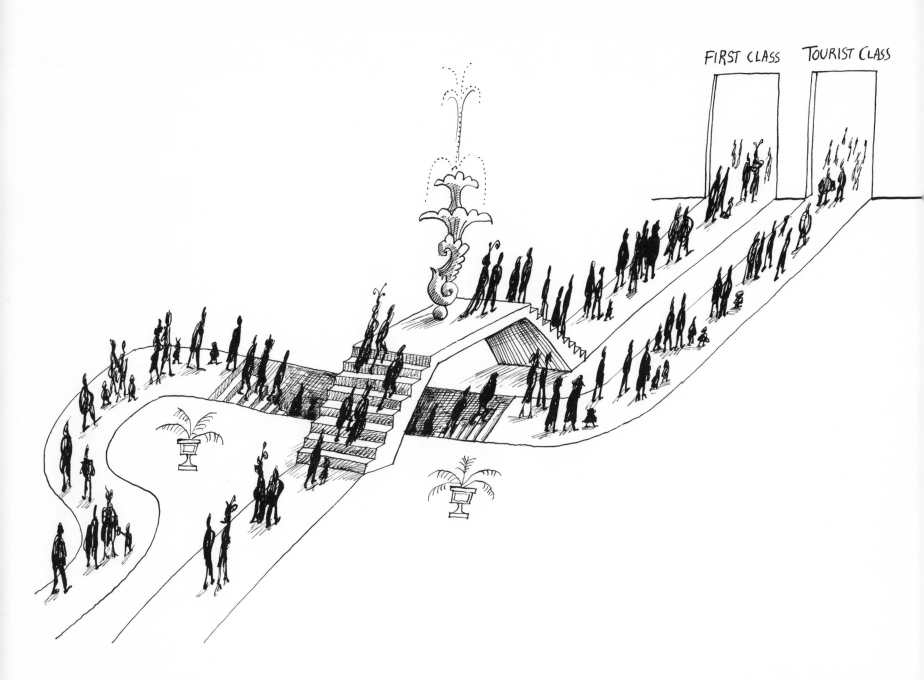

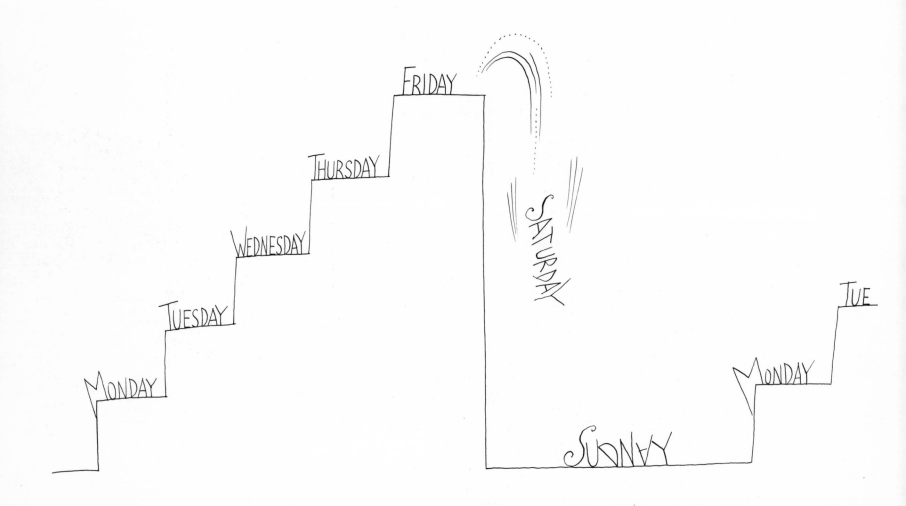

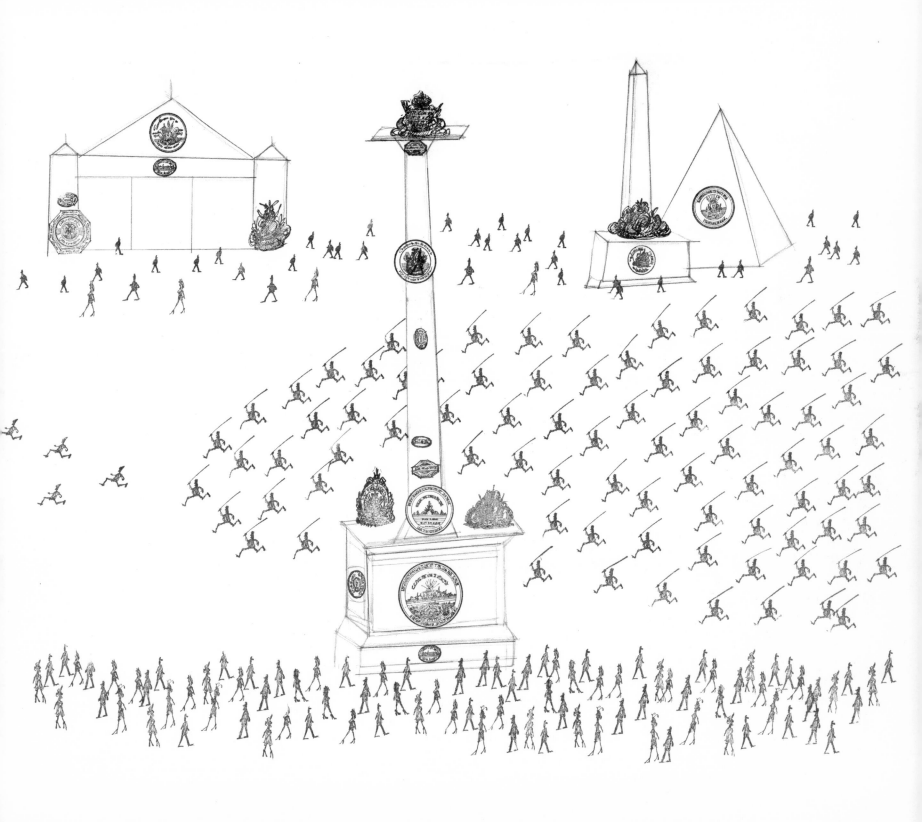

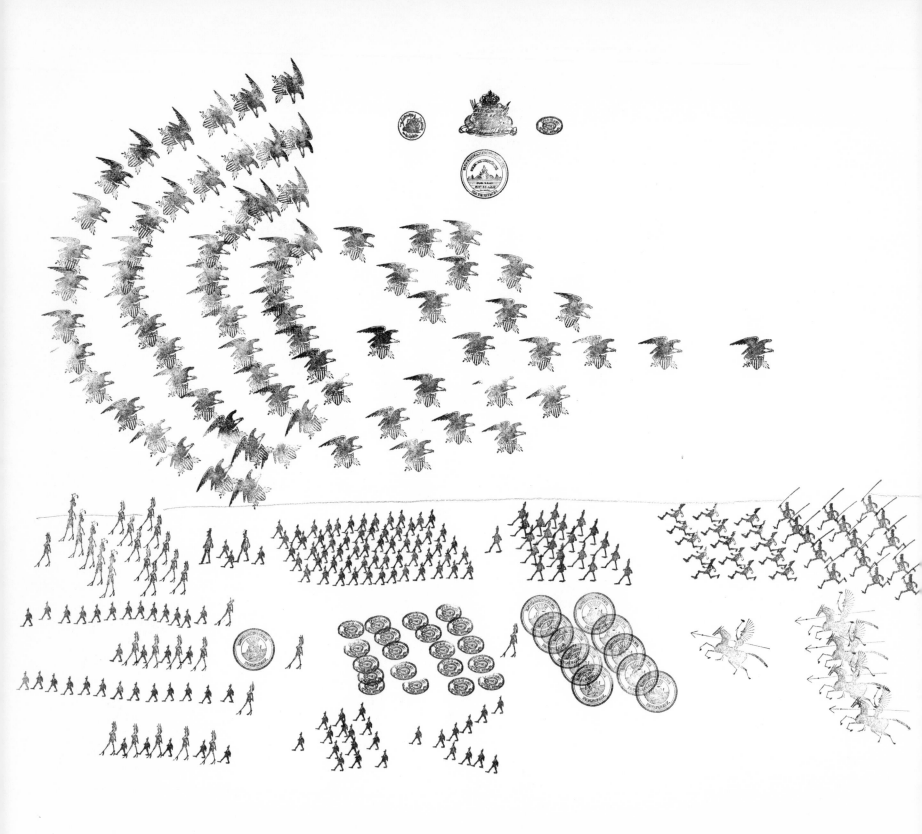

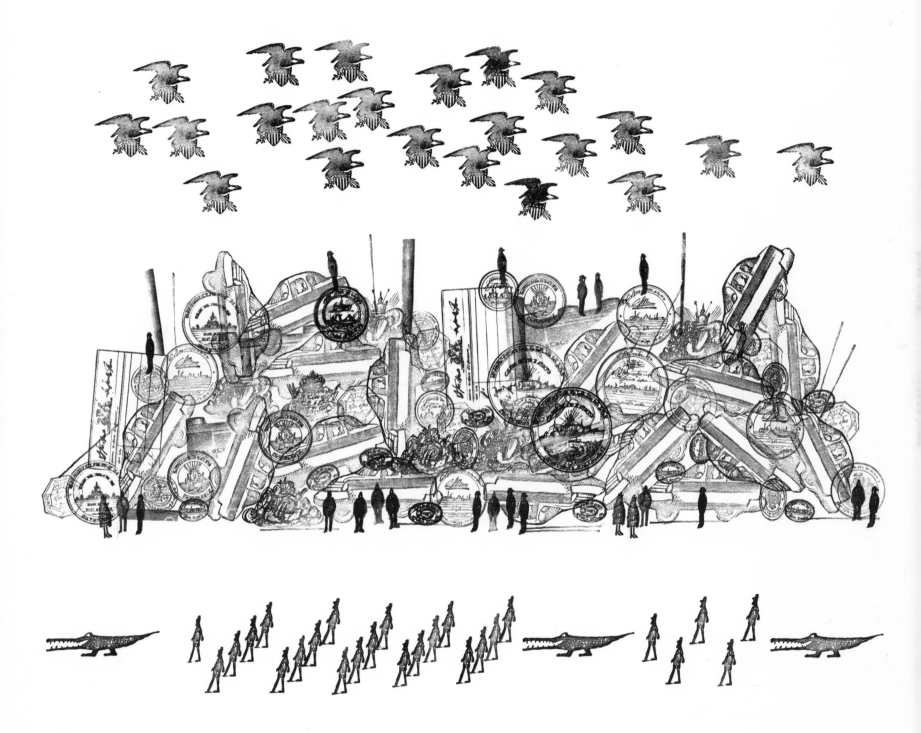

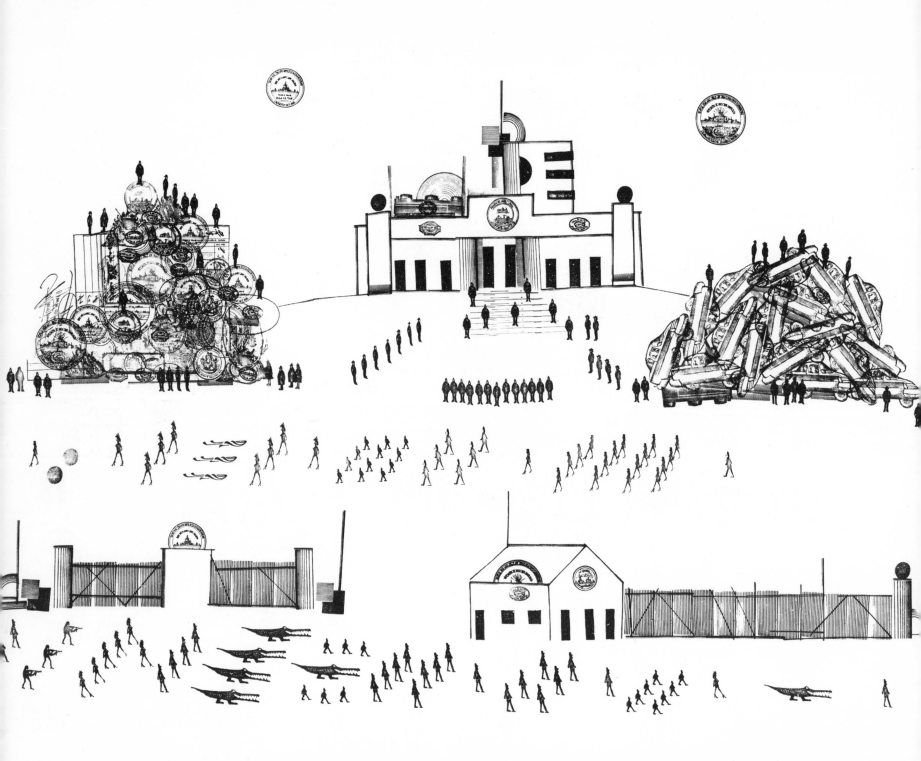

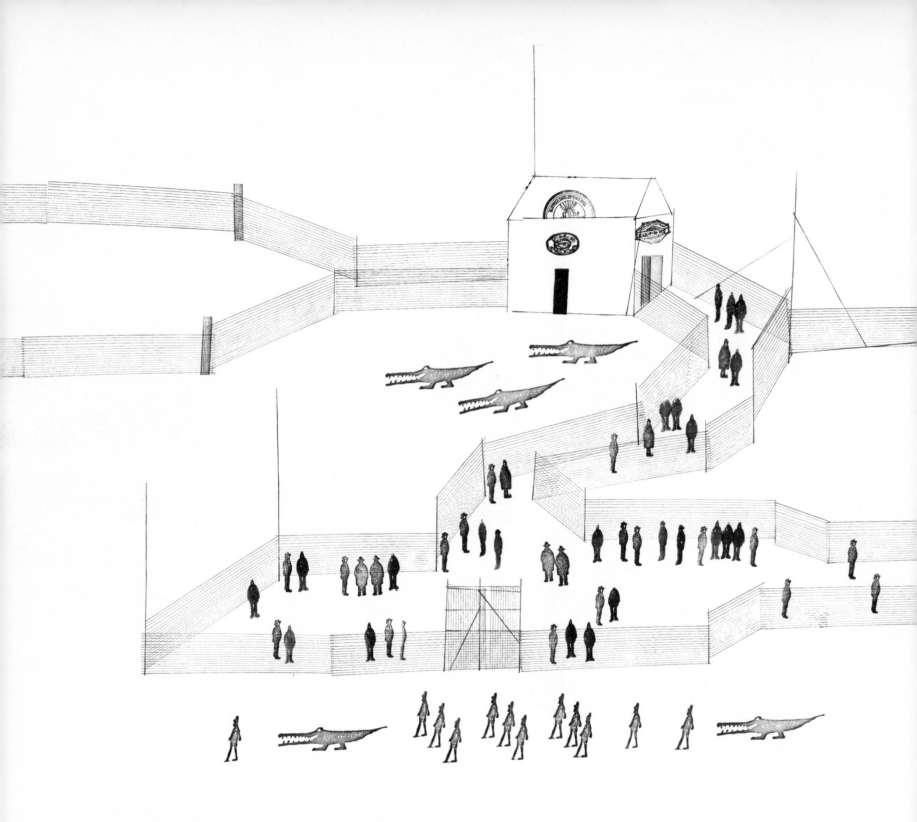

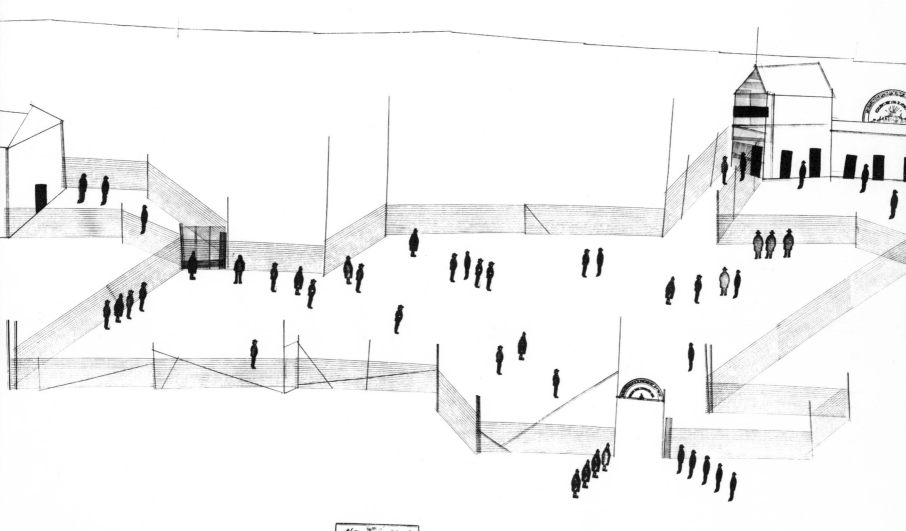

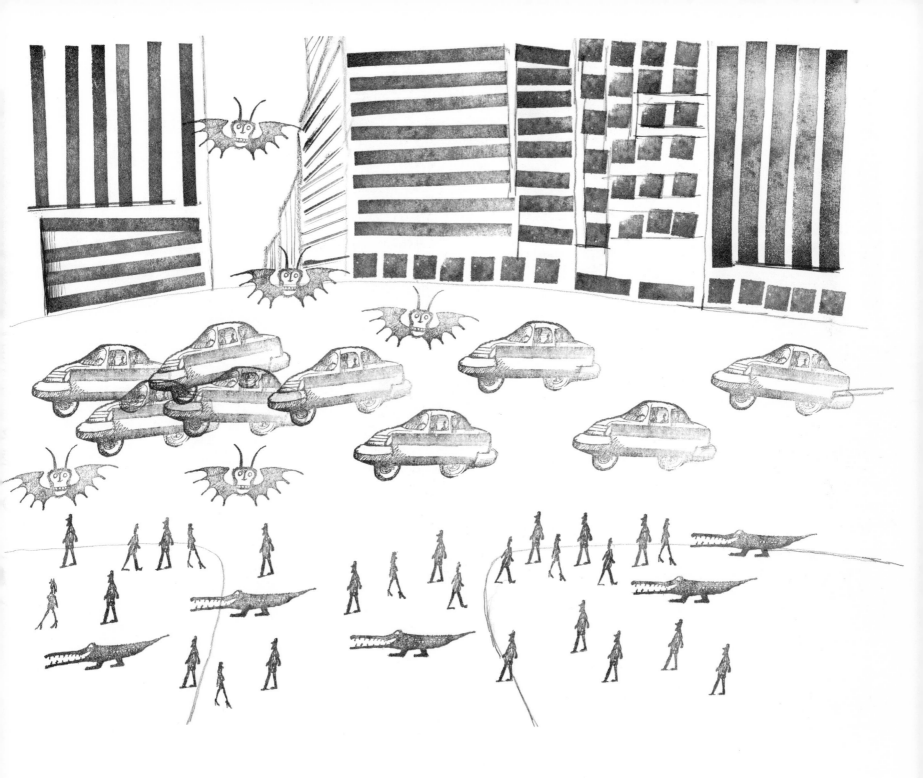

Detroit and Canada Tunnel, near American Portal, Detroit, Mich.   26

Photo Courtesy of Holden, McKinney & Clark

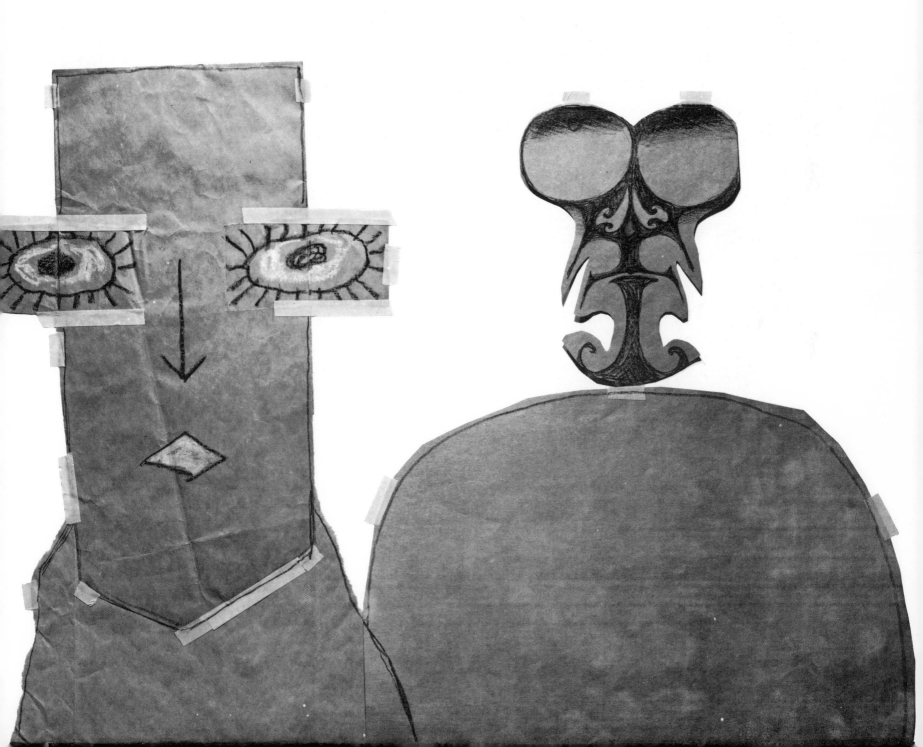

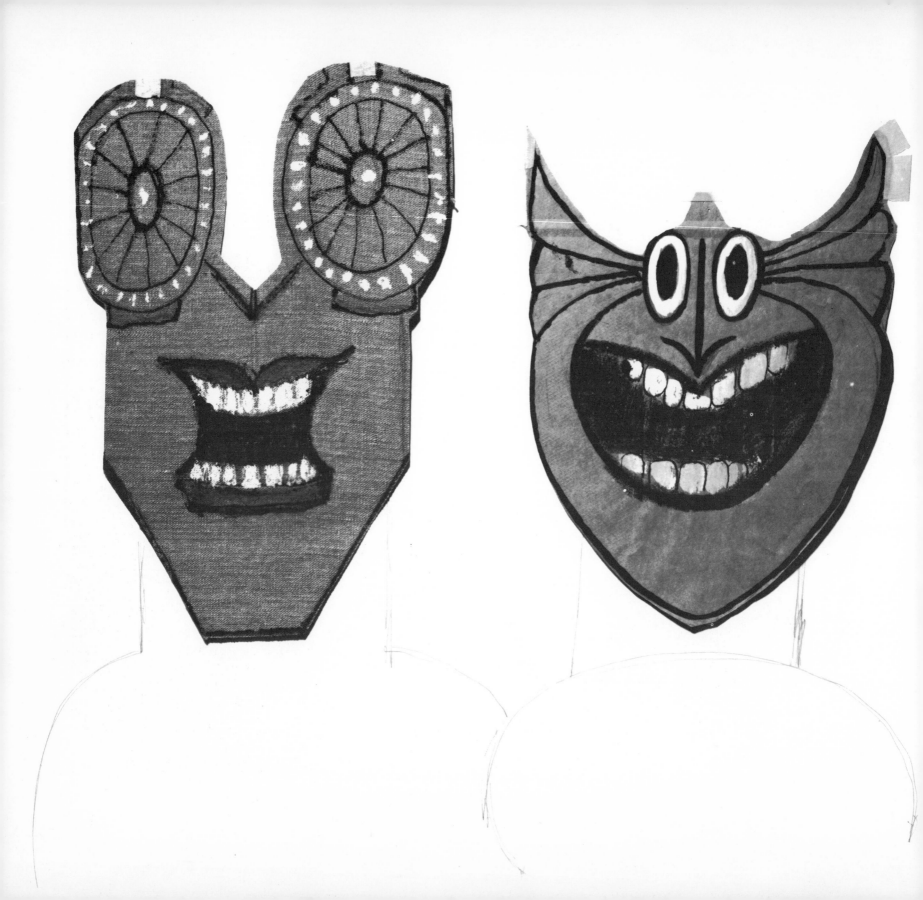

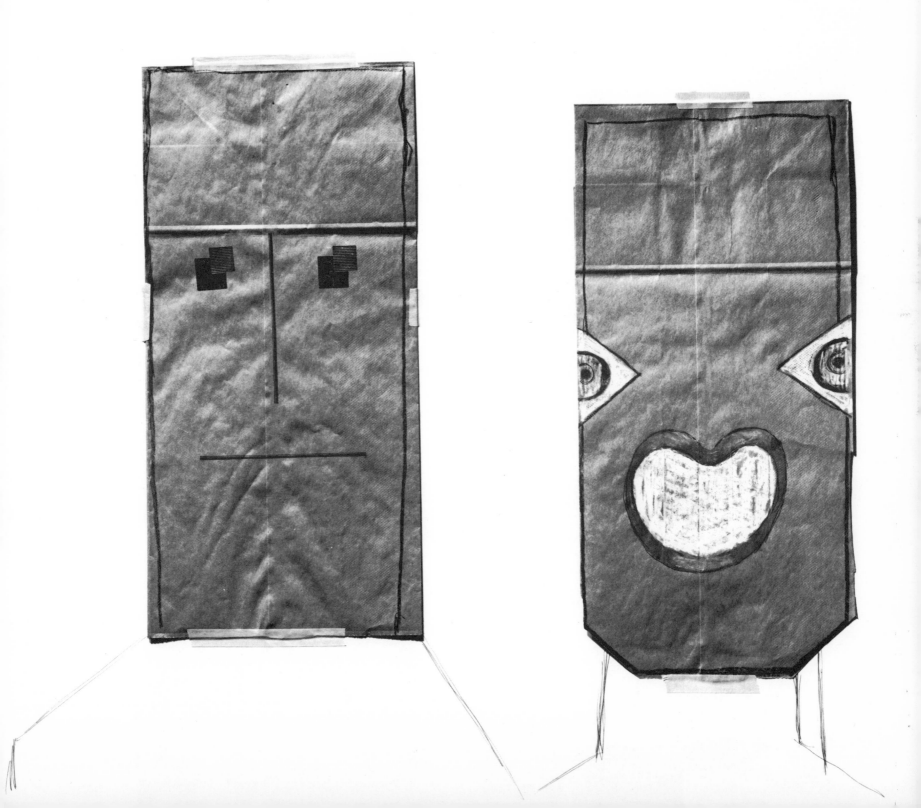

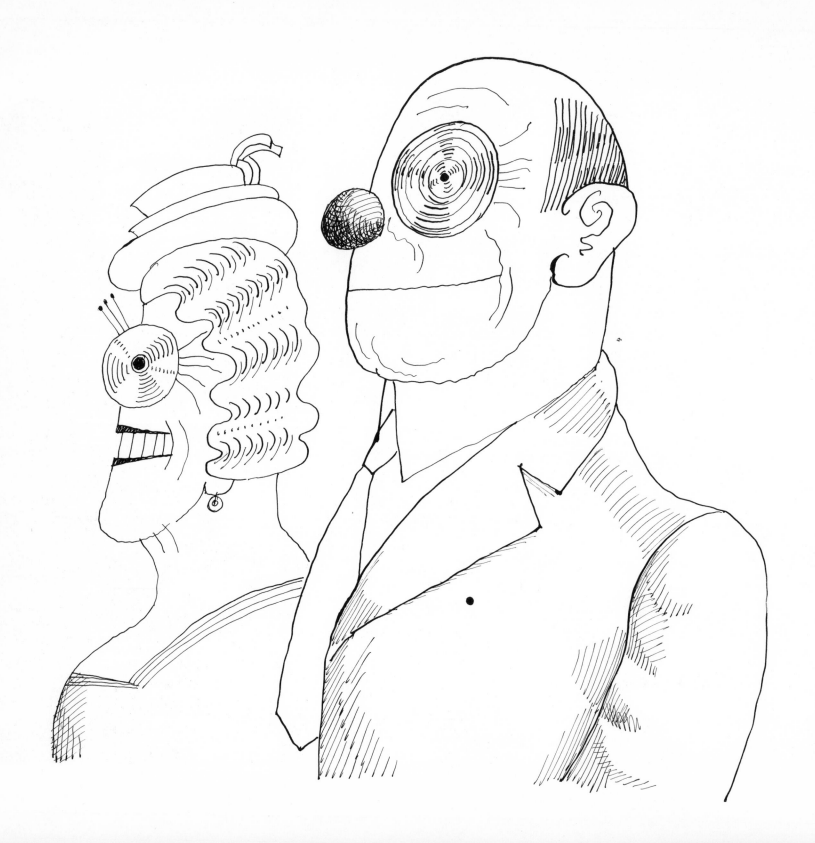

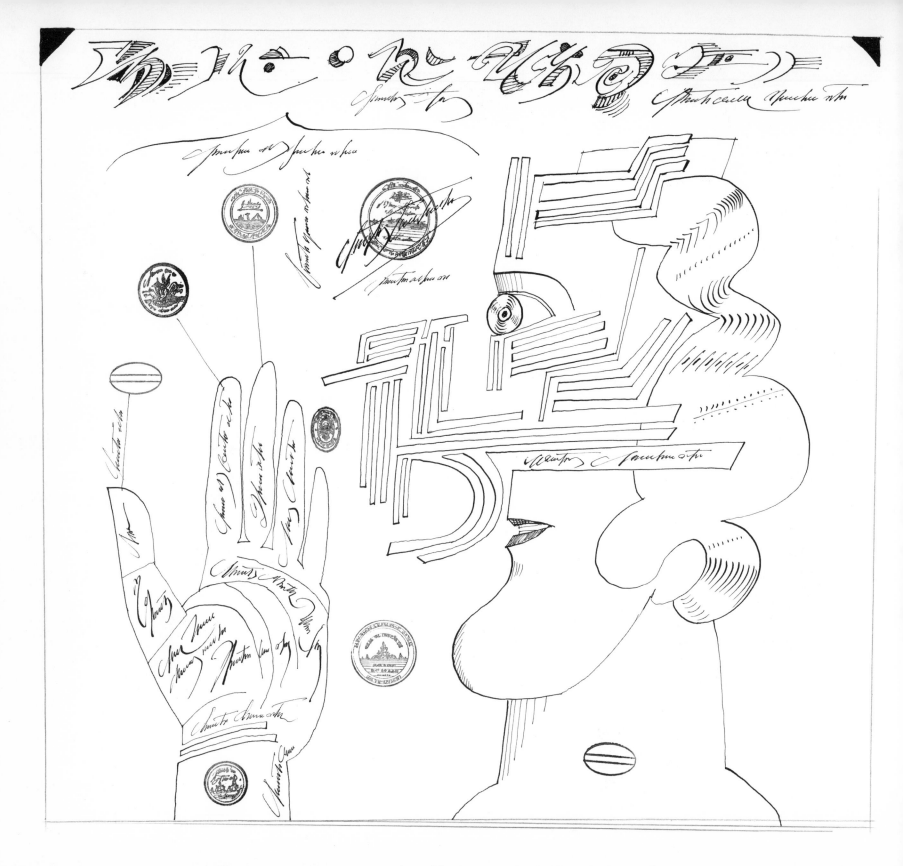

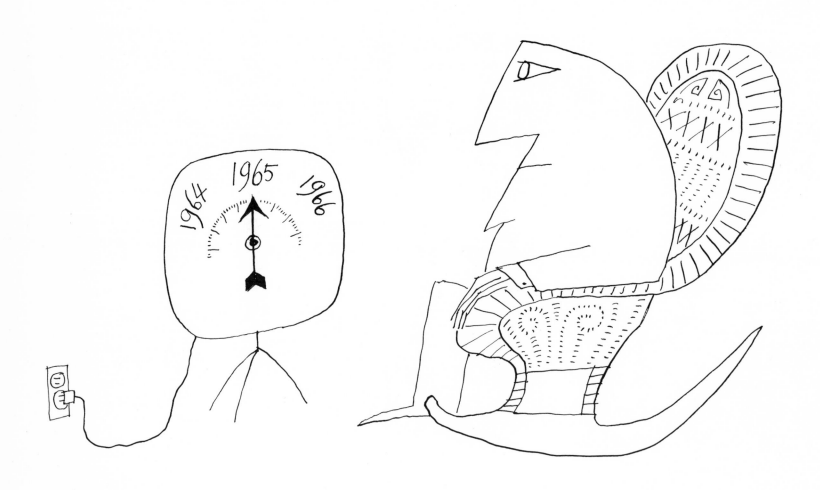

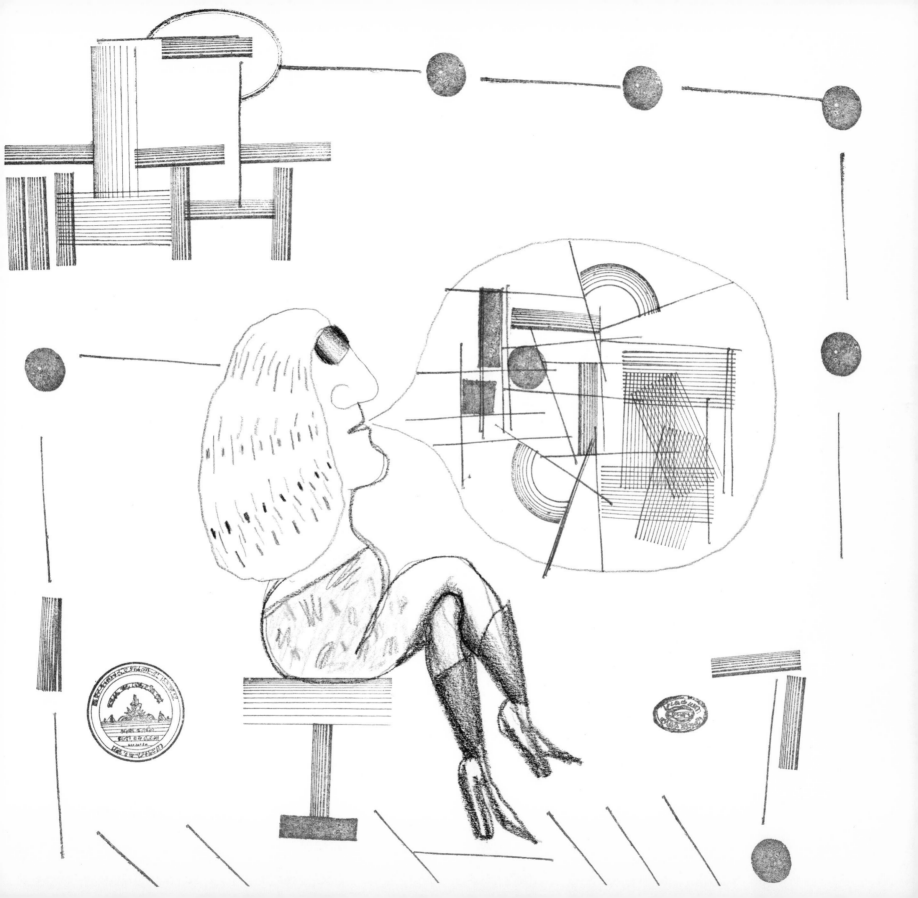

STEINBERG

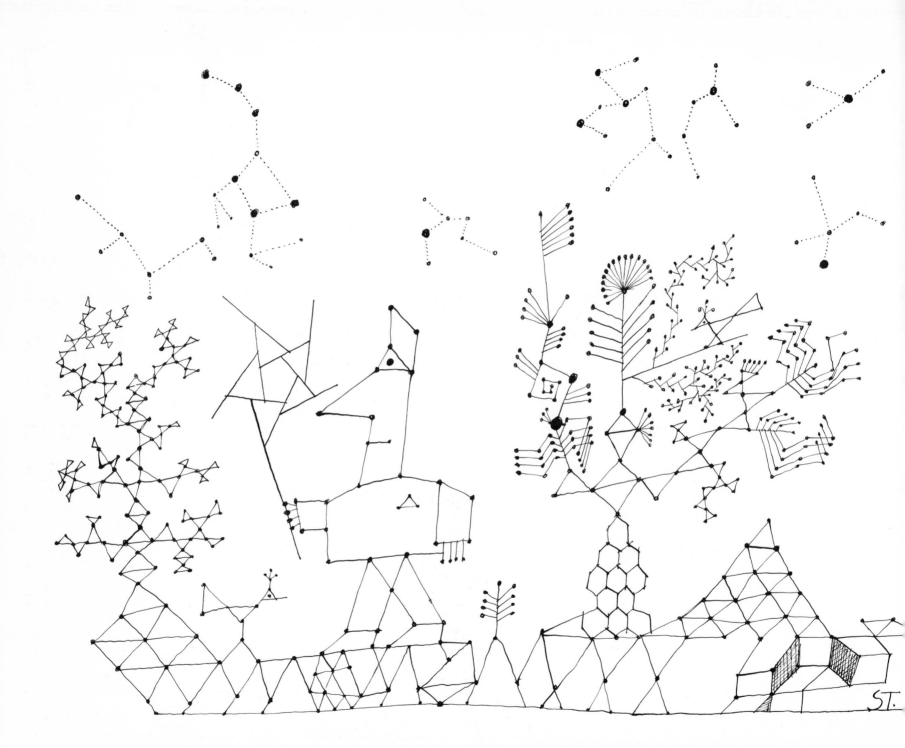

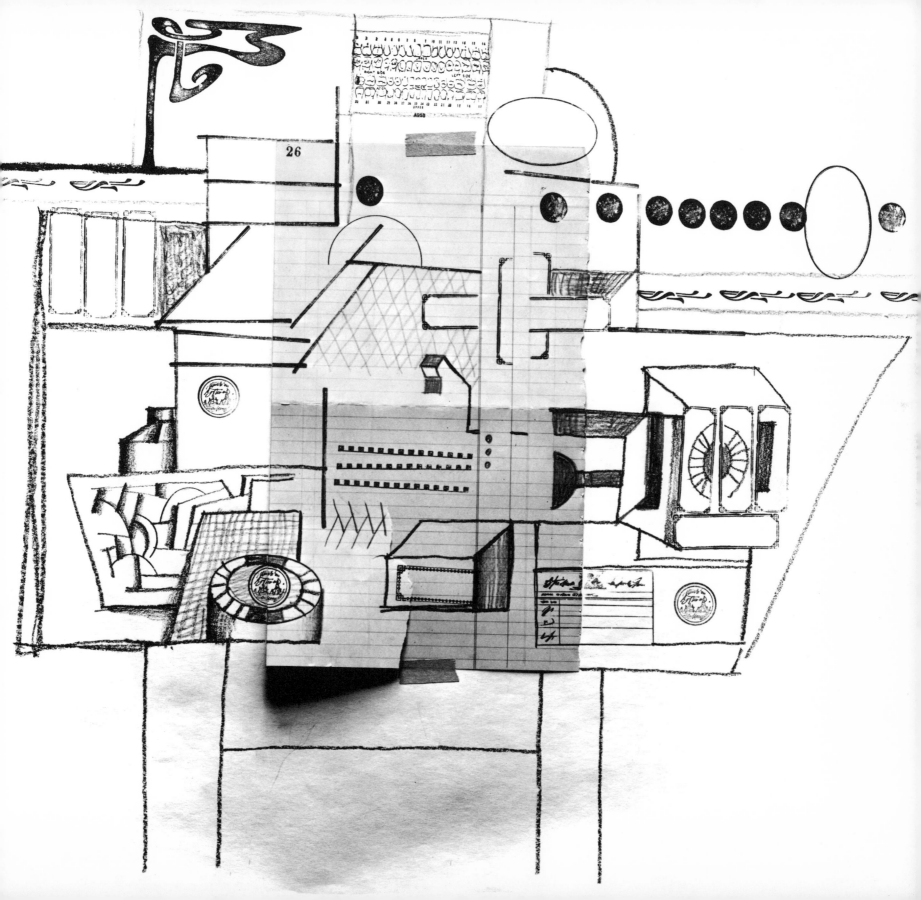

STEINBERG
68

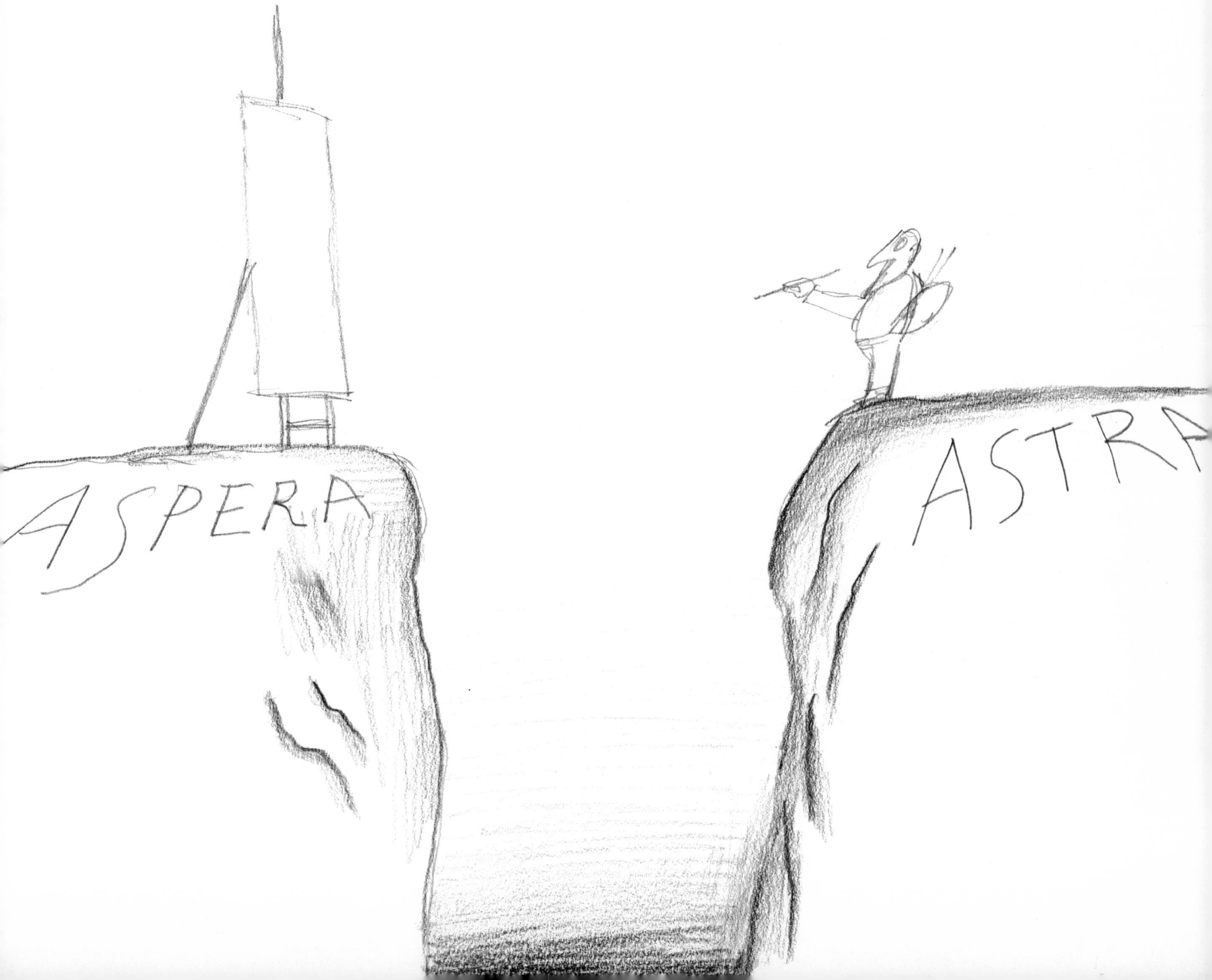
ASPERA
ASTRA

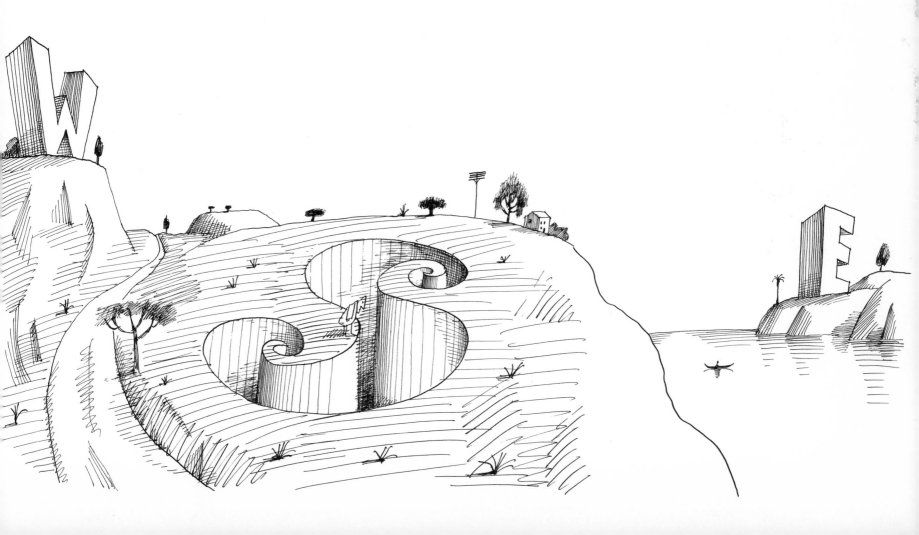

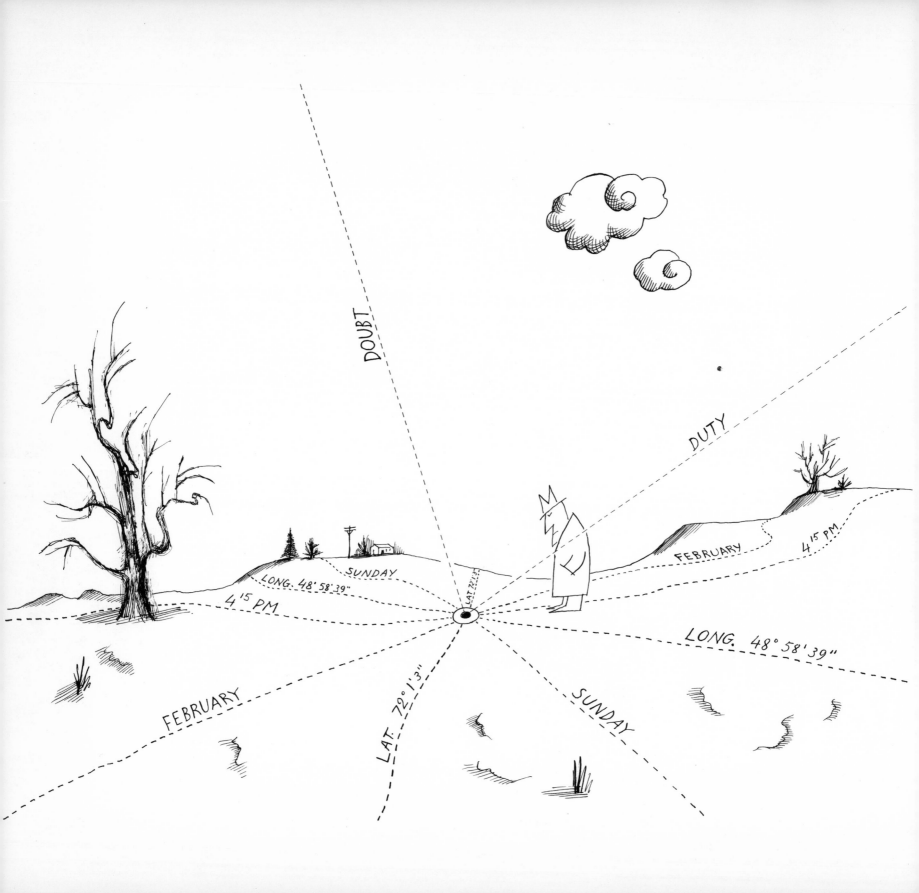

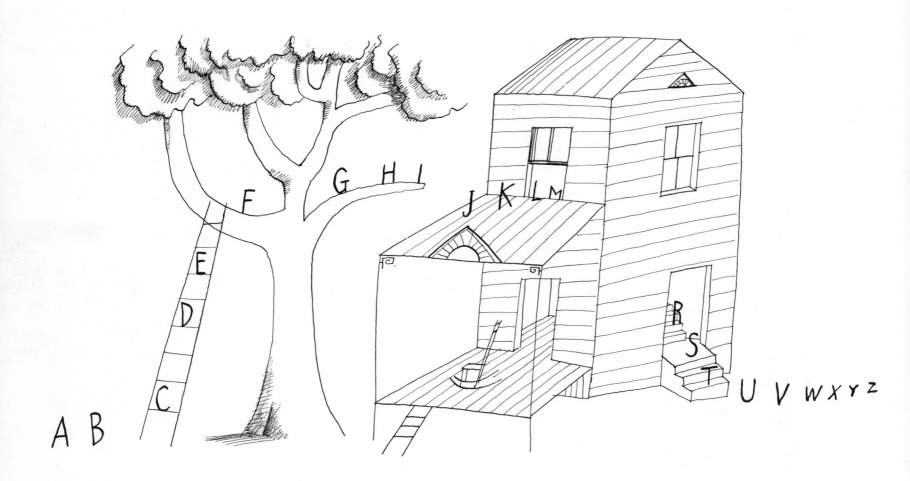

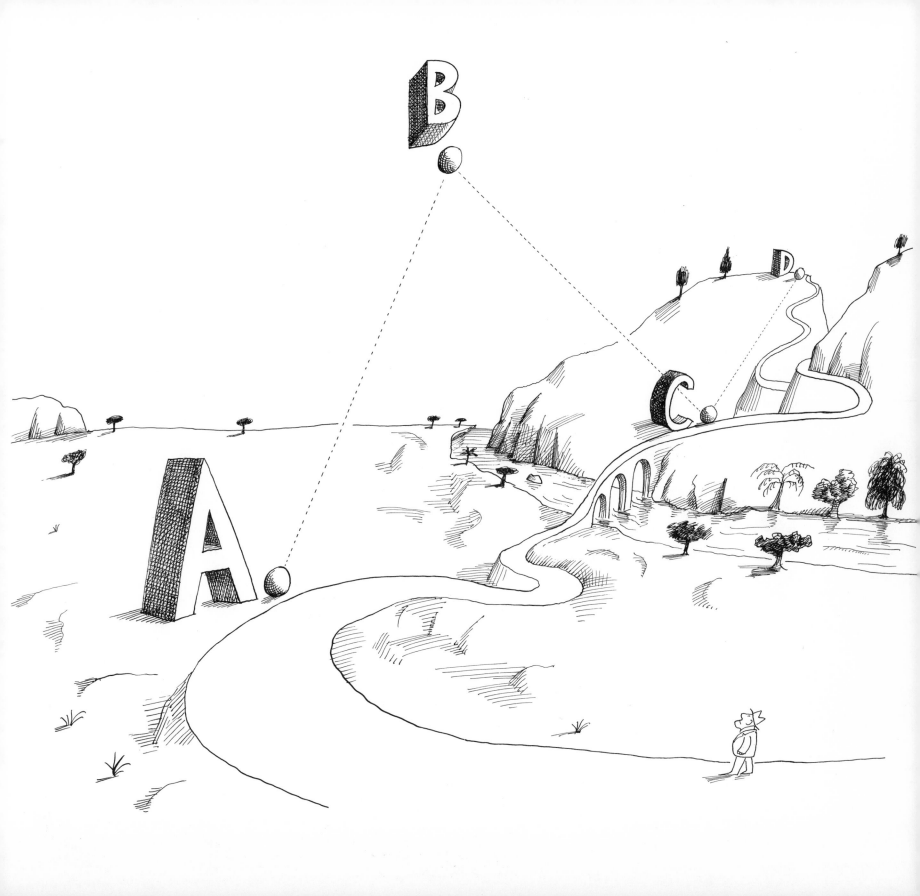

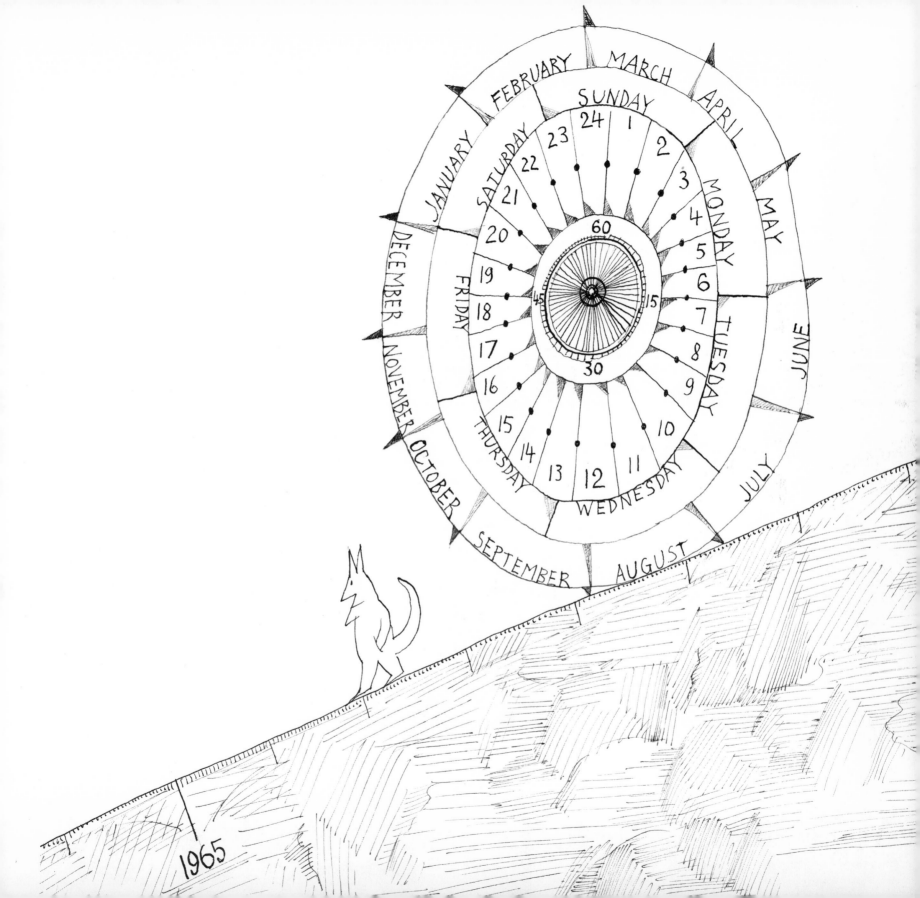

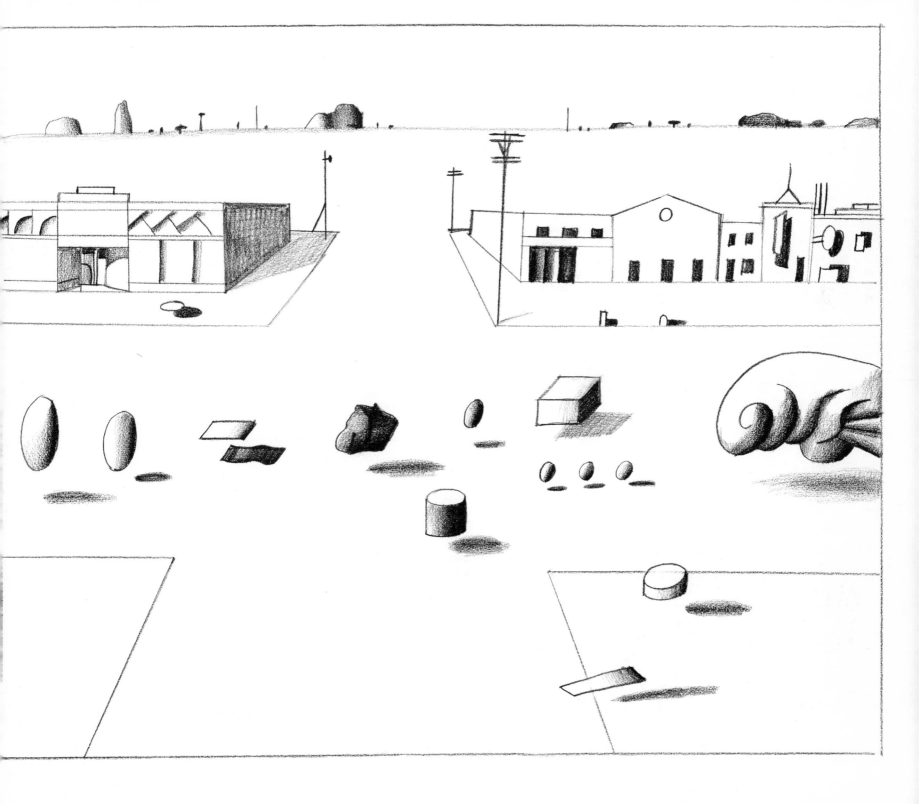

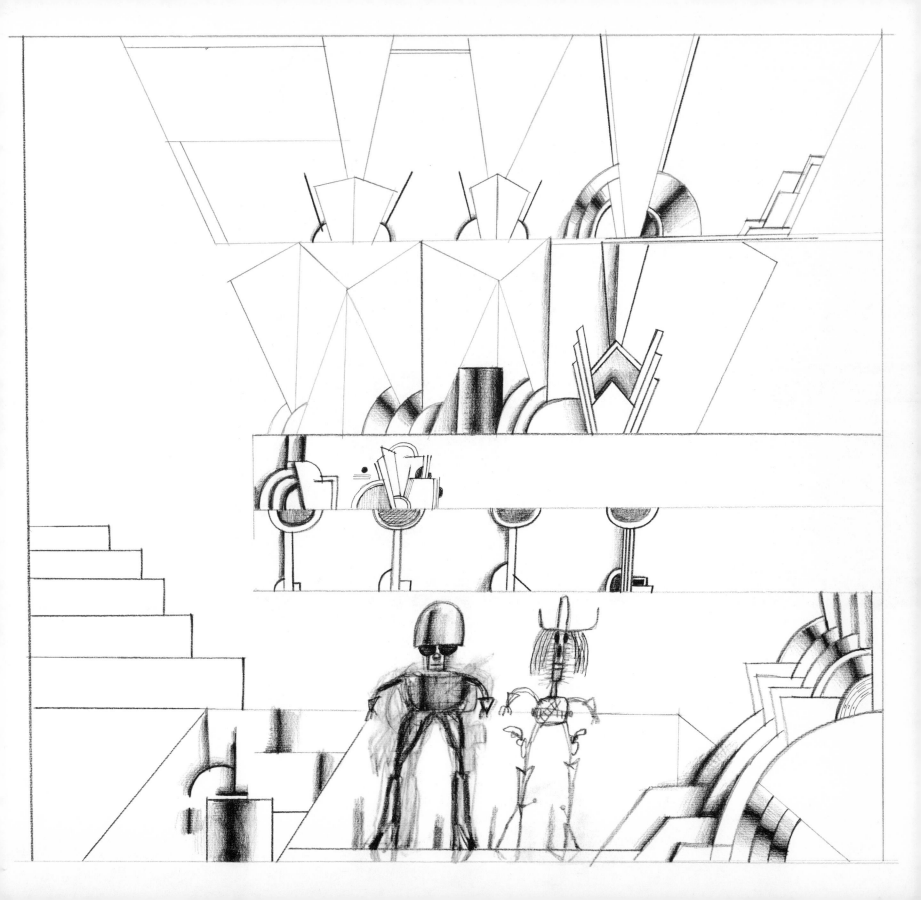

STEINBERG
1970

¡VIVAN!
LAS
CADENAS

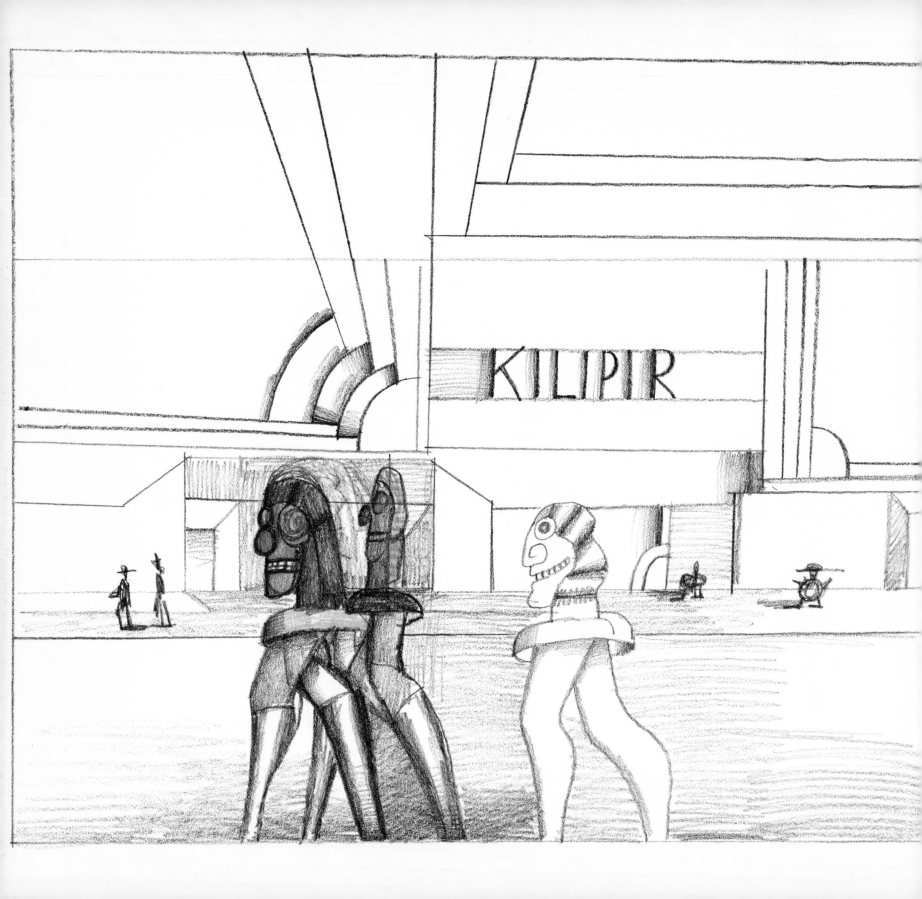

402 — Papeete TAHITI
425 — MARTINIQUE
589 — OAHU
640 — Honolulu ZANZIBAR

10632 — ALBANIA

3275 — LAKE TITICACA

9925 — SICILY

13433 — HOLLAND

34813 — CALABRIA

Taranto BASILICATA CAMPANIA LAZIO Roma
Napoli
PUGLIA ABRUZZI
Bari

7836 — NEW JERSEY Newark

15944 — Atlantic City
Zurich
SWITZERLAND

Cody

WYOMING

97914 sq. mi.

Laramie
Cheyenne

97914 sq. mi.

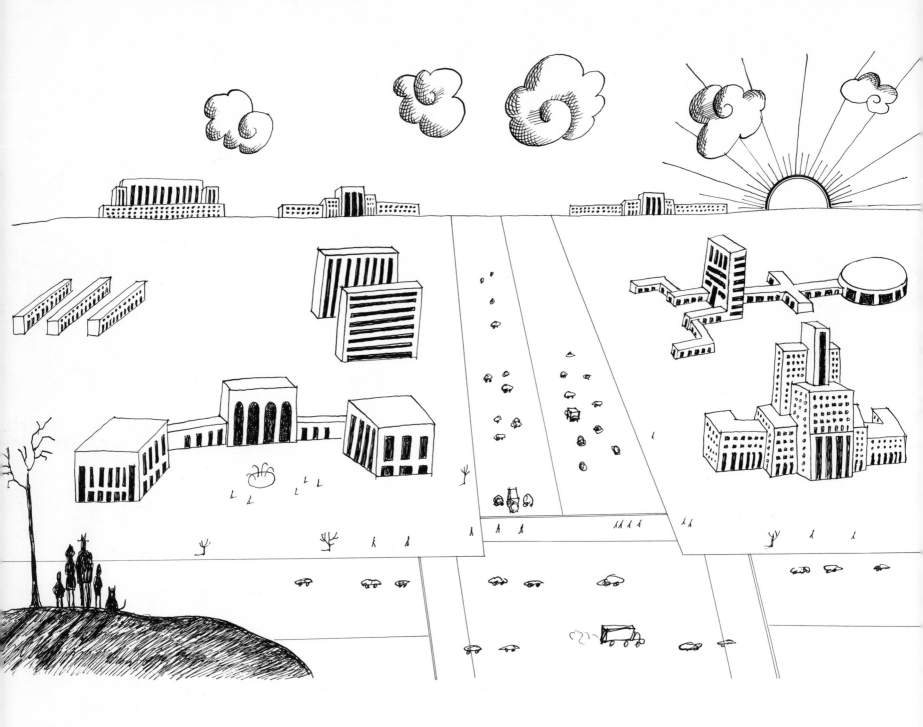

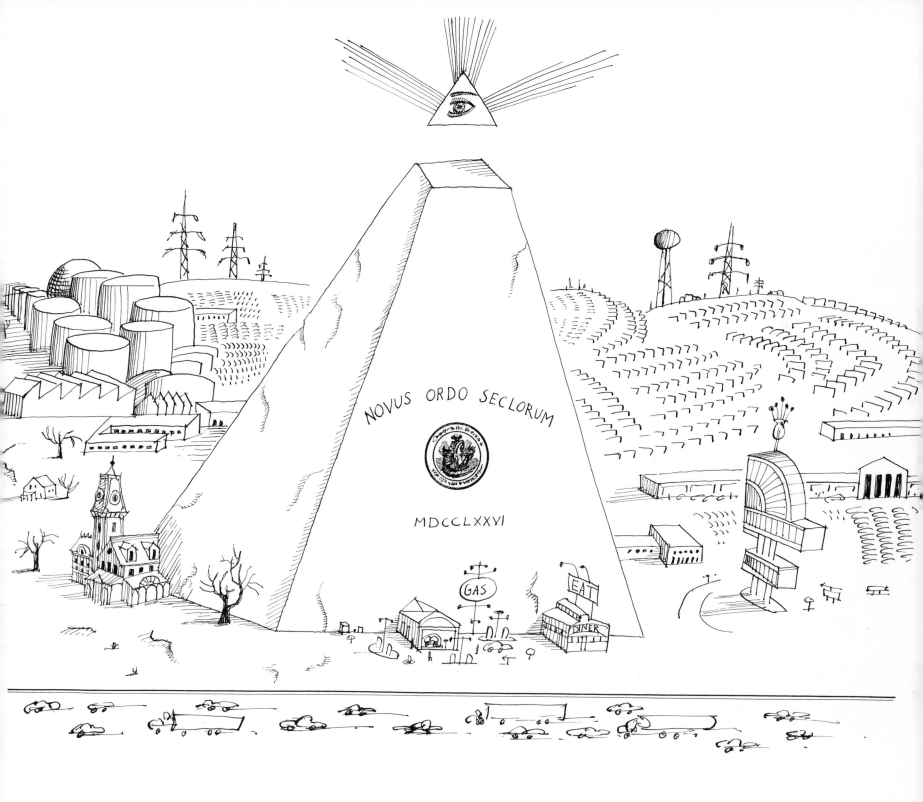

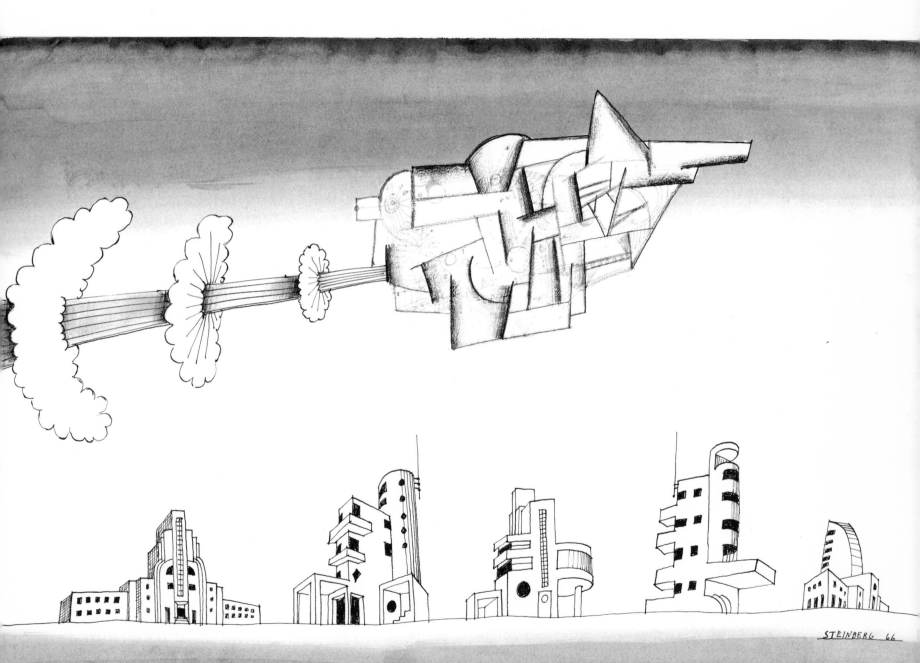

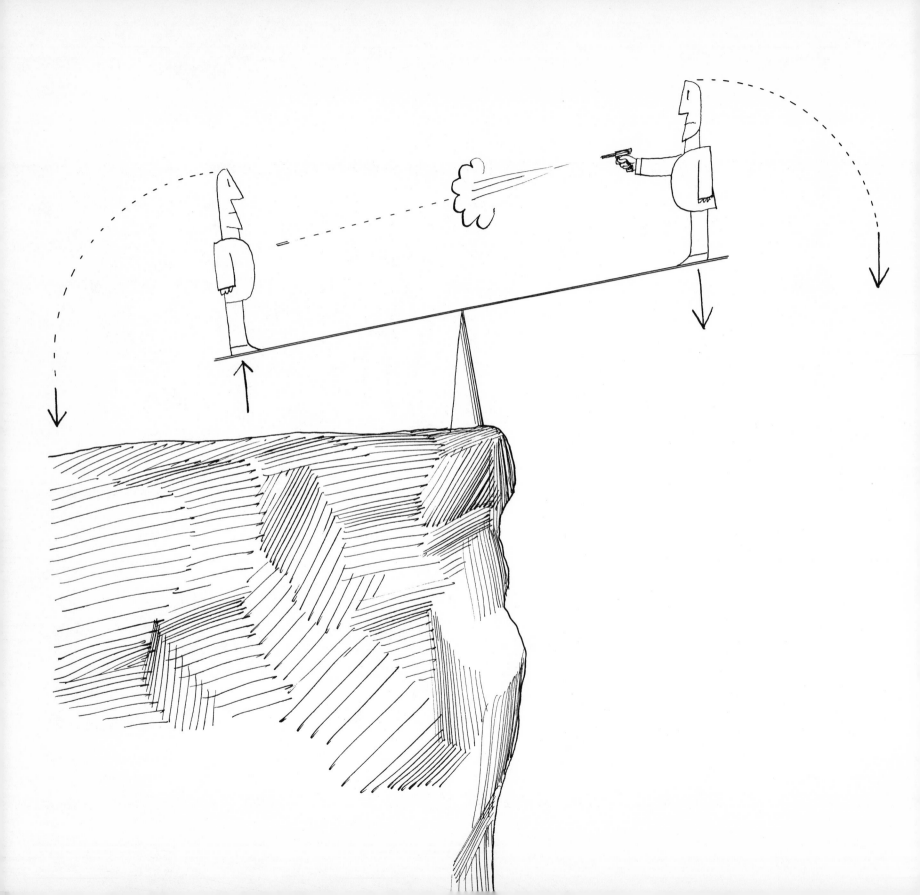

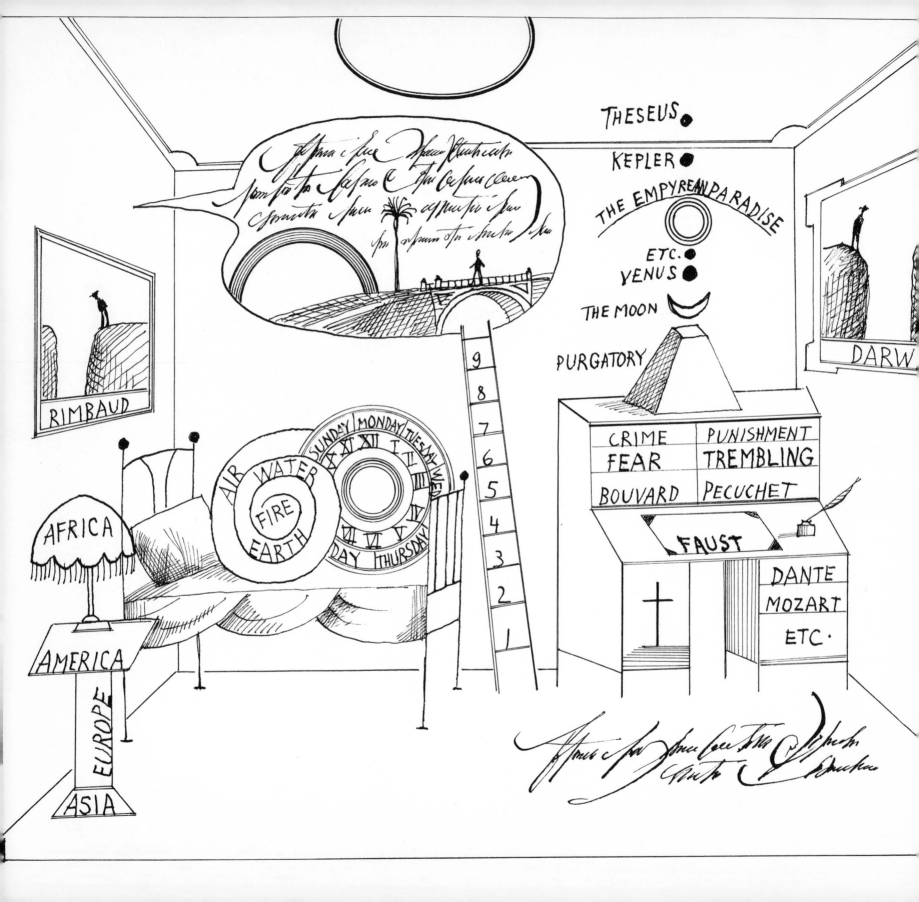

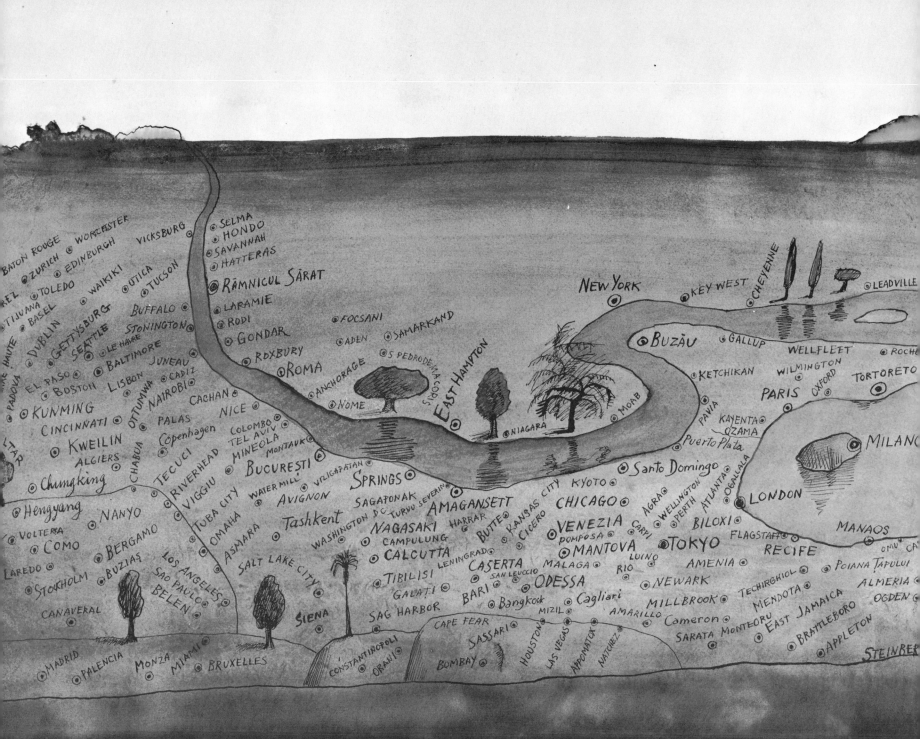

STEINBERG

STEINBERG
ARE WE?
TO BE
I WAS
I SHALL
I WILL!
I AM
WE ARE
I would
I SHOULD

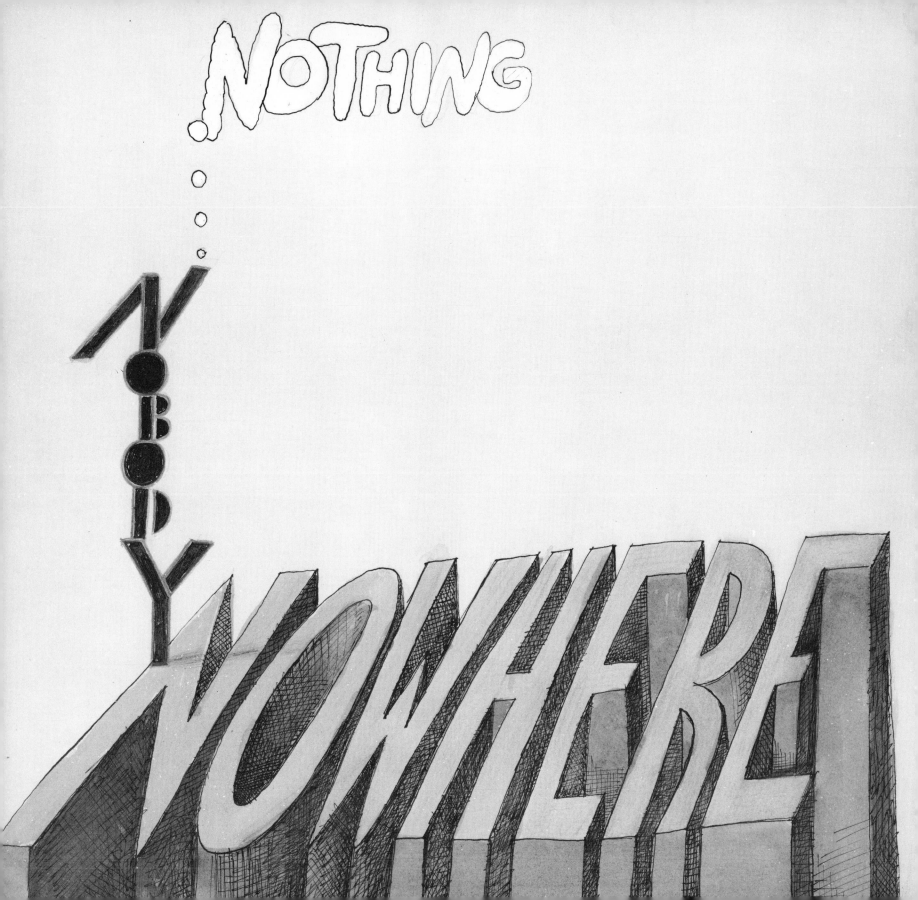

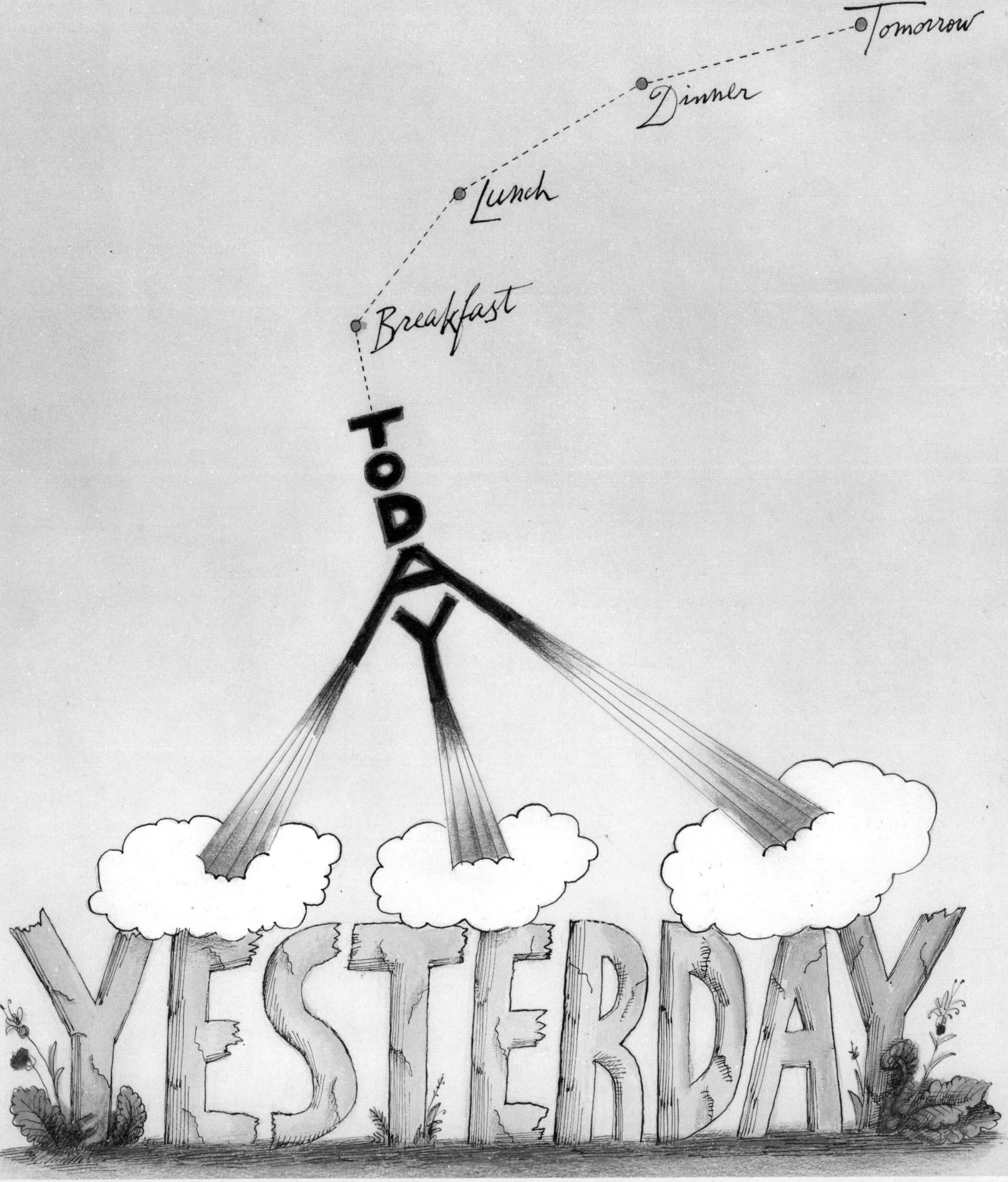
Tomorrow
Dinner
Lunch
Breakfast
TODAY
YESTERDAY

ANNUIT CŒPTIS

STEINBERG 1967